Learning to Read, Step by Step!

Ready to Read   Preschool–Kindergarten
• big type and easy words • rhyme and rhythm • picture clues
For children who know the alphabet and are eager to begin reading.

Reading with Help   Preschool–Grade 1
• basic vocabulary • short sentences • simple stories
For children who recognize familiar words and sound out new words with help.

Reading on Your Own   Grades 1–3
• engaging characters • easy-to-follow plots • popular topics
For children who are ready to read on their own.

Reading Paragraphs   Grades 2–3
• challenging vocabulary • short paragraphs • exciting stories
For newly independent readers who read simple sentences with confidence.

Ready for Chapters   Grades 2–4
• chapters • longer paragraphs • full-color art
For children who want to take the plunge into chapter books but still like colorful pictures.

STEP INTO READING® is designed to give every child a successful reading experience. The grade levels are only guides; children will progress through the steps at their own speed, developing confidence in their reading.

Remember, a lifetime love of reading starts with a single step!

The authors would like to thank Kaitlin Dupuis and Deanna Ellis for their help in creating this book.

Text copyright © 2019 by Kratt Brothers Company Ltd.

All rights reserved. Published in the United States by Random House Children's Books, a division of Penguin Random House LLC, 1745 Broadway, New York, NY 10019, and in Canada by Penguin Random House Canada Limited, Toronto.

Wild Kratts® © 2019 Kratt Brothers Company Ltd. / 9 Story Media Group Inc. Wild Kratts®, Creature Power® and associated characters, trademarks, and design elements are owned by Kratt Brothers Company Ltd. Licensed by Kratt Brothers Company Ltd.

Step into Reading, Random House, and the Random House colophon are registered trademarks of Penguin Random House LLC.

Visit us on the Web!
StepIntoReading.com
rhcbooks.com

Educators and librarians, for a variety of teaching tools, visit us at
RHTeachersLibrarians.com

ISBN 978-1-101-93914-7 (trade) — ISBN 978-1-101-93915-4 (lib. bdg.) —
ISBN 978-1-101-93916-1 (ebook)

Printed in the United States of America
10 9 8 7 6 5 4 3 2 1

WILD KRATTS

Wild Cats!

by Martin Kratt and Chris Kratt

Random House 🏠 New York

Wild Cats

Big or small, wild or tame,
cats are one of the Wild Kratts'
favorite predators.

Members of the cat family
are smart, fast, and strong.
And those are just a few
of their Creature Powers!

Cats Around the World

There are 38 species
of wild cats in the world.

lion   tiger

There are big wild cats,
such as **lions** and **tigers**.

There are medium-sized wild cats,
such as **lynxes** and **caracals**.

lynx

caracal

There are even small ones,
such as **margays**
and **African wildcats**.

margay

African wildcat

Cubs and Kittens

The young of big cats

are called **cubs**.

The young of medium

and small cats

are called **kittens**.

Mother cats care for their young
and teach them how to hunt.

How Cats Hunt

Cats are very good hunters. Some cats rely on speed to hunt. Others use their size and strength.

Cats have sharp claws, sharp teeth, and powerful jaws that help them catch their prey.

Shhh . . . quiet. Now pounce!

Big Wild Cats

Lions live in savannas

and dry forests.

They are one of the biggest cats.

They mostly hunt big mammals,
such as zebras and wildebeests.
Lions often hunt in groups
to take down animals that
a single lion could not.

That's teamwork!

Medium Wild Cats

Caracals are great jumpers!

Their main prey is birds.

Their cousin, the **serval**,
hunts rodents
and other small prey.
Both of these cats live in
the same areas as lions.

Orange and Black Stripes!

Many types of cats have stripes, but the **tiger** is the most famous. Their stripes hide them in the forest shadows while they hunt.

Spot the Cat

Like stripes, spots help cats such as **ocelots** blend in with their surroundings.

Ocelots are very good tree climbers.

They hunt lizards, monkeys, and other small prey.

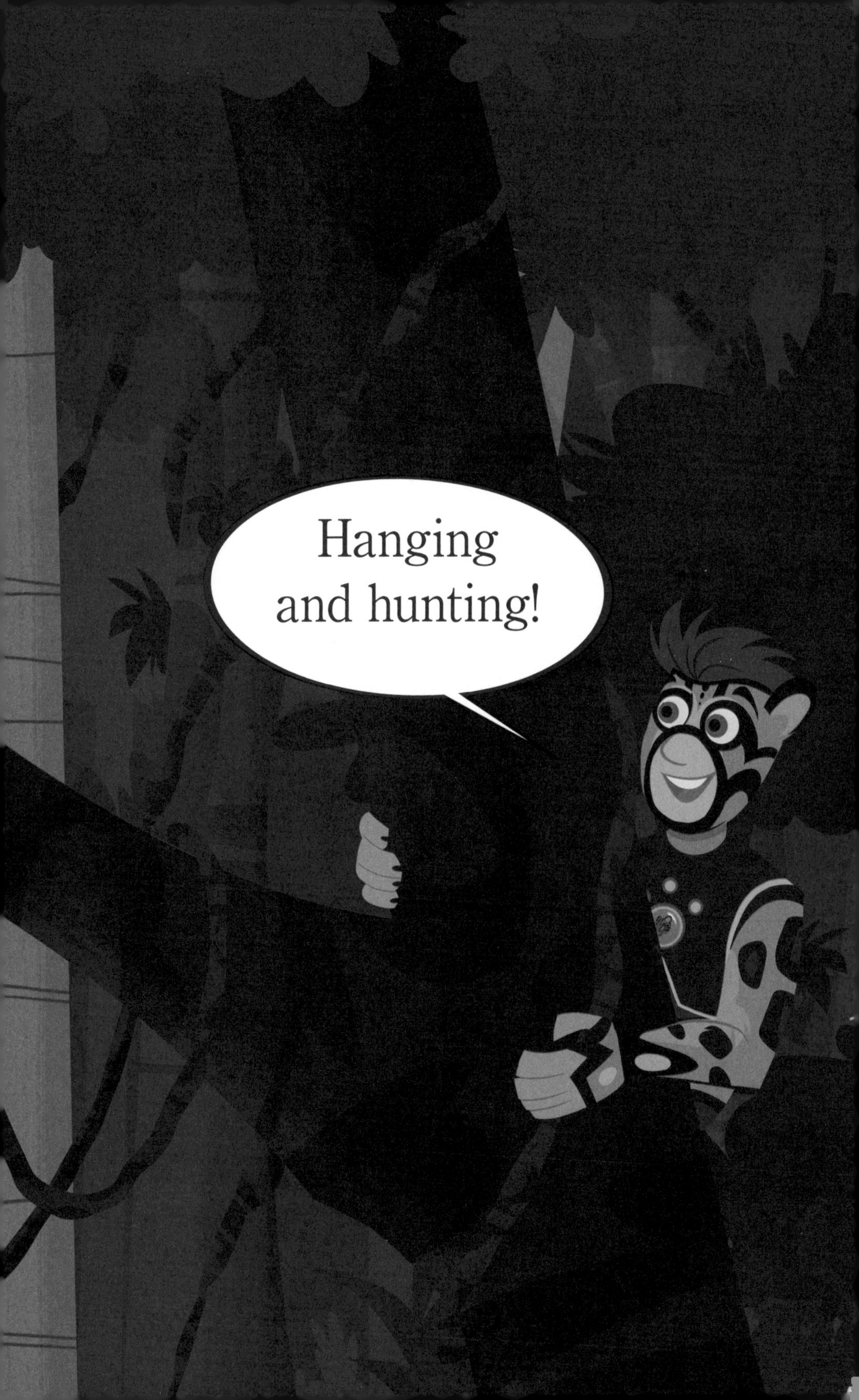
Hanging and hunting!

Spotted Speedsters

Cheetahs are the fastest
of all cats.
Their bodies have evolved
to run at great speeds.

Unlike most cats, their claws always stick out a little to grip the ground when they run.

We're at top speed—65 miles per hour!

Versatile Hunters

Jaguars are stocky and muscular.
They mostly live in the jungles
of Central and South America.
They hunt on land and in the water.

Leopards are lean and muscular.

They live in Asia and Africa.

They climb high into trees

to keep their food

away from lions.

Big Foot

Furry **lynxes** often live

in very cold areas.

Their big feet enable them

to run on top of the snow.

Their prey include hares, rabbits,

and other small creatures.

We have
big feet
too!

I'm still going to catch you!

Name Game

Mountain lions live in
the Americas.
They have many habitats,
ranging from the desert
to snowy mountains.
They also have different names
in different places . . .

The **Florida panther** is a type of mountain lion.
It has been known to clash with another fierce predator—the alligator!

There are less than
250 Florida panthers
left in the wild.
They may soon
disappear forever.

Some wild cats, such as
the Caspian tiger, have died out.
Bengal tigers are endangered,
and cheetah numbers are
declining.

Wild cats are amazing creatures.
Humans should try to help
wild cats survive so we can
always find them out there . . .